Gertrude Chandler Warner's

THE BOXCAR CHILDREN GRAPHIC NOVELS

THE HAUNTED CABIN MYSTERY

Henry, Jessie, Violet, and Benny take a trip down the Mississippi River in a paddle-wheel boat and stay in a haunted cabin! At least it seems haunted—there are spooky phone calls, flickering lights, and strange shadows. Are there really ghosts, or is someone trying to scare the Boxcar Children away?

THE BOXCAR CHILDREN
GRAPHIC NOVELS

THE BOXCAR CHILDREN
SURPRISE ISLAND
THE YELLOW HOUSE MYSTERY
MYSTERY RANCH
MIKE'S MYSTERY
BLUE BAY MYSTERY
SNOWBOUND MYSTERY
TREE HOUSE MYSTERY
THE HAUNTED CABIN MYSTERY

Gertrude Chandler Warner's

THE BOXCAR CHILDREN
THE HAUNTED CABIN MYSTERY

Adapted by Jeff Limke
Illustrated by Mark Bloodworth

Henry Alden

Watch

Jessie Alden

Violet Alden

Benny Alden

Visit us at www.albertwhitman.com.

Adapted by Jeff Limke
Illustrated by Mark Bloodworth
Colored by Carlos Badilla
Lettered by Johnny Lowe
Edited by Stephanie Hedlund
Interior layout and design by Kristen Fitzner Denton
Cover art by Mike Dubisch
Book design and packaging by Shannon Eric Denton

Library of Congress Cataloging-in-Publication Data
is available from the Library of Congress.

THE HAUNTED CABIN MYSTERY

Contents

The Telegram 6
Cap and Doodle 8
Weird Noises, Strange Lights 11
Will-o'-the-Wisp 13
Scrambled Eggs 15
The Carpenter 18
Storm Clouds 20
Henry's Plan 23
Caught! 25
The Real Treasure 28
The Final Surprise 30

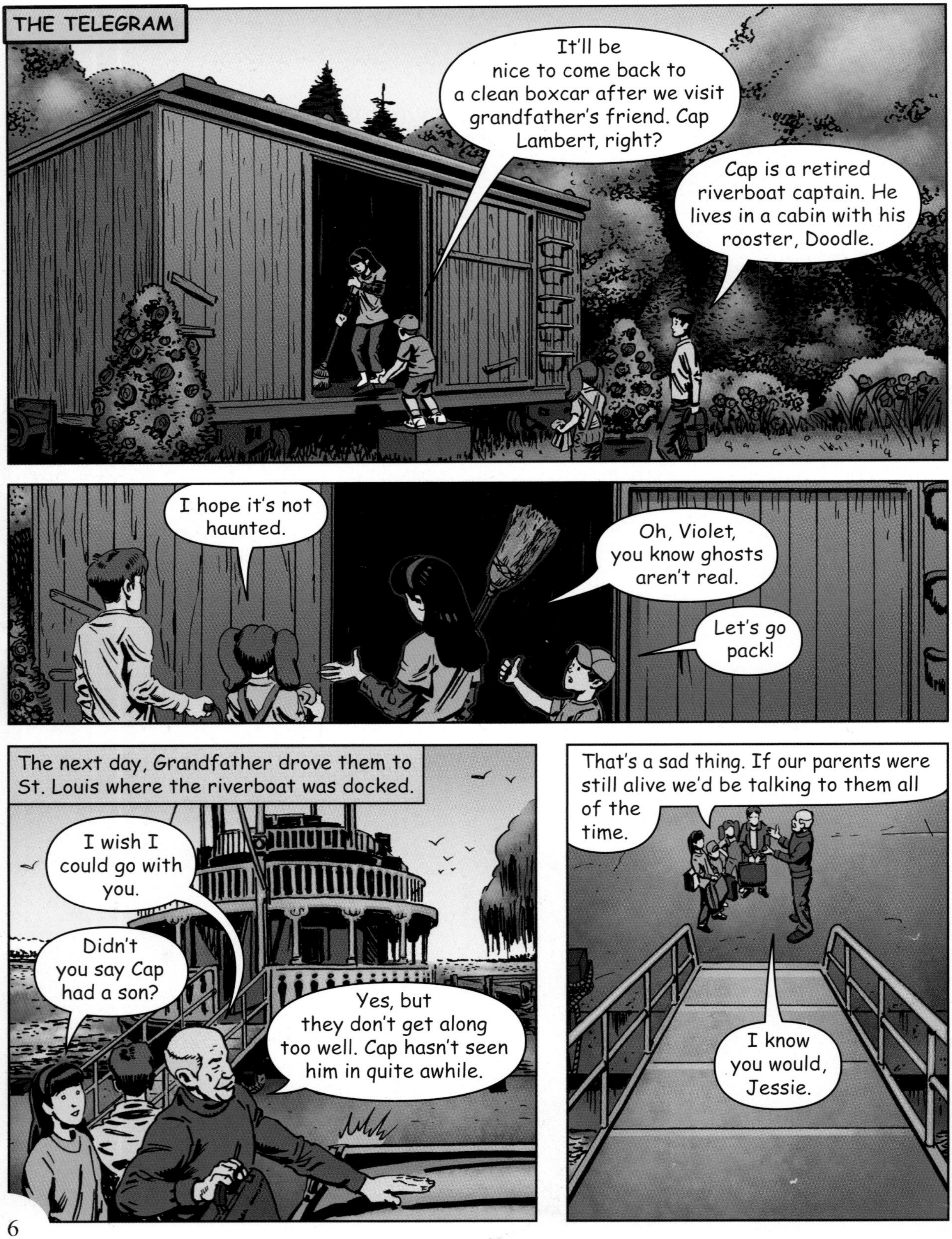
THE TELEGRAM
It'll be nice to come back to a clean boxcar after we visit grandfather's friend. Cap Lambert, right?
Cap is a retired riverboat captain. He lives in a cabin with his rooster, Doodle.
I hope it's not haunted.
Oh, Violet, you know ghosts aren't real.
Let's go pack!
The next day, Grandfather drove them to St. Louis where the riverboat was docked.
I wish I could go with you.
Didn't you say Cap had a son?
Yes, but they don't get along too well. Cap hasn't seen him in quite awhile.
That's a sad thing. If our parents were still alive we'd be talking to them all of the time.
I know you would, Jessie.

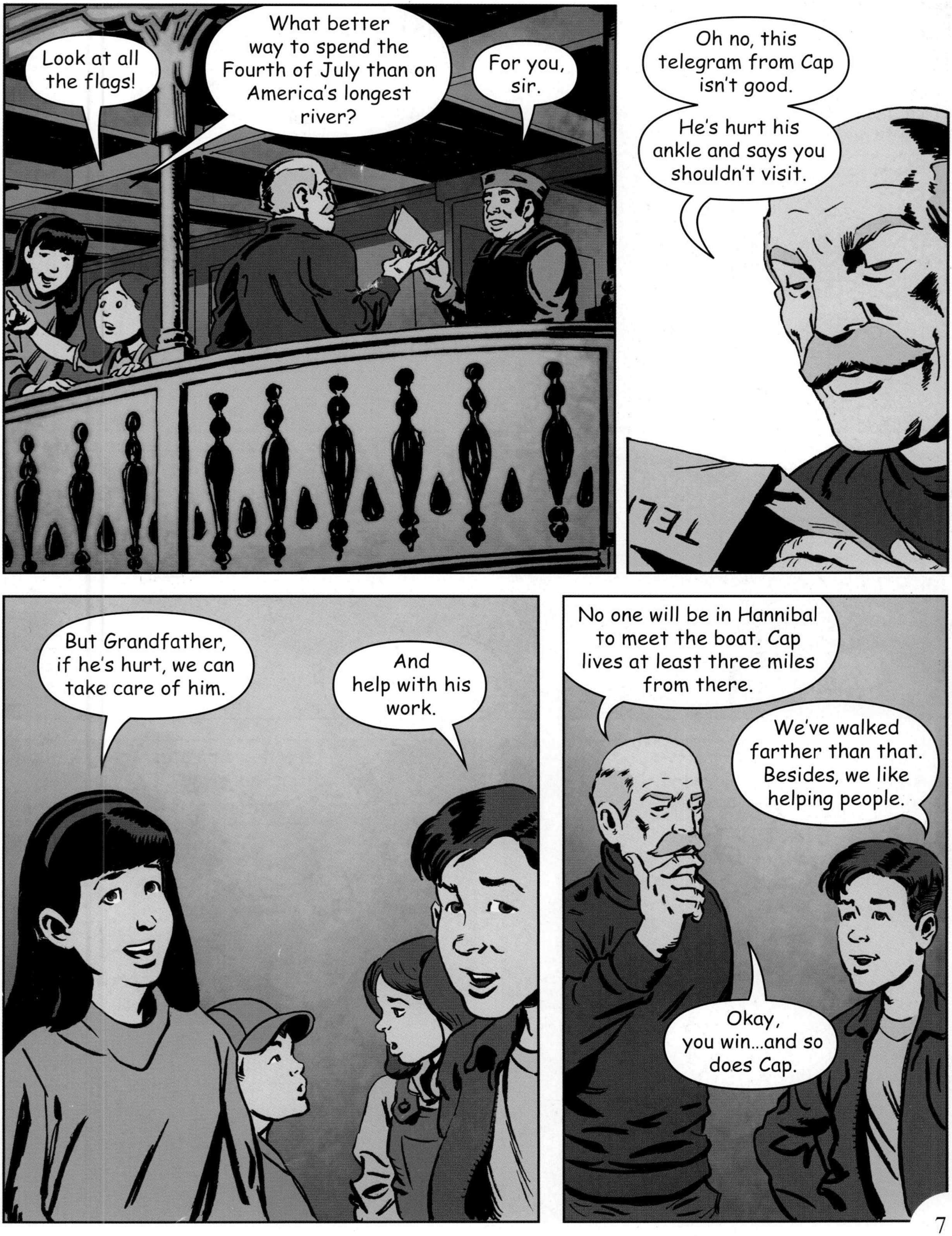
Look at all the flags!
What better way to spend the Fourth of July than on America's longest river?
For you, sir.
Oh no, this telegram from Cap isn't good.
He's hurt his ankle and says you shouldn't visit.
TEL
But Grandfather, if he's hurt, we can take care of him.
And help with his work.
No one will be in Hannibal to meet the boat. Cap lives at least three miles from there.
We've walked farther than that. Besides, we like helping people.
Okay, you win...and so does Cap.

CAP AND DOODLE

The girls left their luggage in their cabins and went to find the boys.

Excuse me, have you seen two boys, one tall and one short?

You'll find the Alden boys on the top deck.

That Mr. Jay isn't very friendly. Why'd he cover his face?

How did you know his name?

From his name tag.

Come on. It's time to eat!

What a great bridge!

It's the Eads Bridge. I'm Paul Edwards, and you must be the Alden children.

Yes. You must read a lot about bridges.

I do, I also write articles about the river.

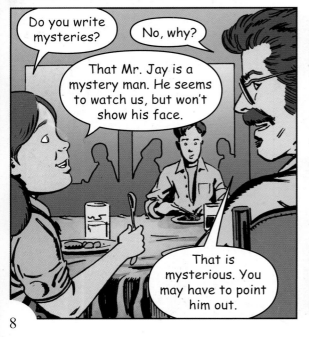

Do you write mysteries?

No, why?

That Mr. Jay is a mystery man. He seems to watch us, but won't show his face.

That is mysterious. You may have to point him out.

Are there pirates on this river?

No, but there are legends of pirate treasure buried around here. I just wrote a story in the paper about it.

8

The next day, the Aldens tried calling Cap to let him know they had arrived.

Cap's phone is disconnected.

Oh, that's not good. If he's injured, he needs a phone.

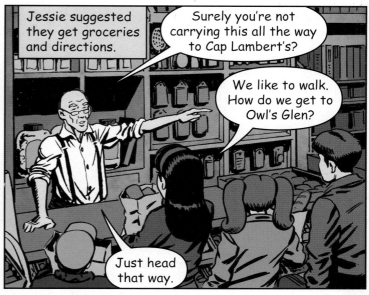

Jessie suggested they get groceries and directions.

Surely you're not carrying this all the way to Cap Lambert's?

We like to walk. How do we get to Owl's Glen?

Just head that way.

Is that Cap's cabin? It looks like it's haunted.

Benny, what an imagination you have.

Hi! You must be Cap Lambert! How'd you get hurt?

Go away, whoever you are!

We're the Aldens.

Didn't you get my message?

We did, but we came to help you anyway.

9

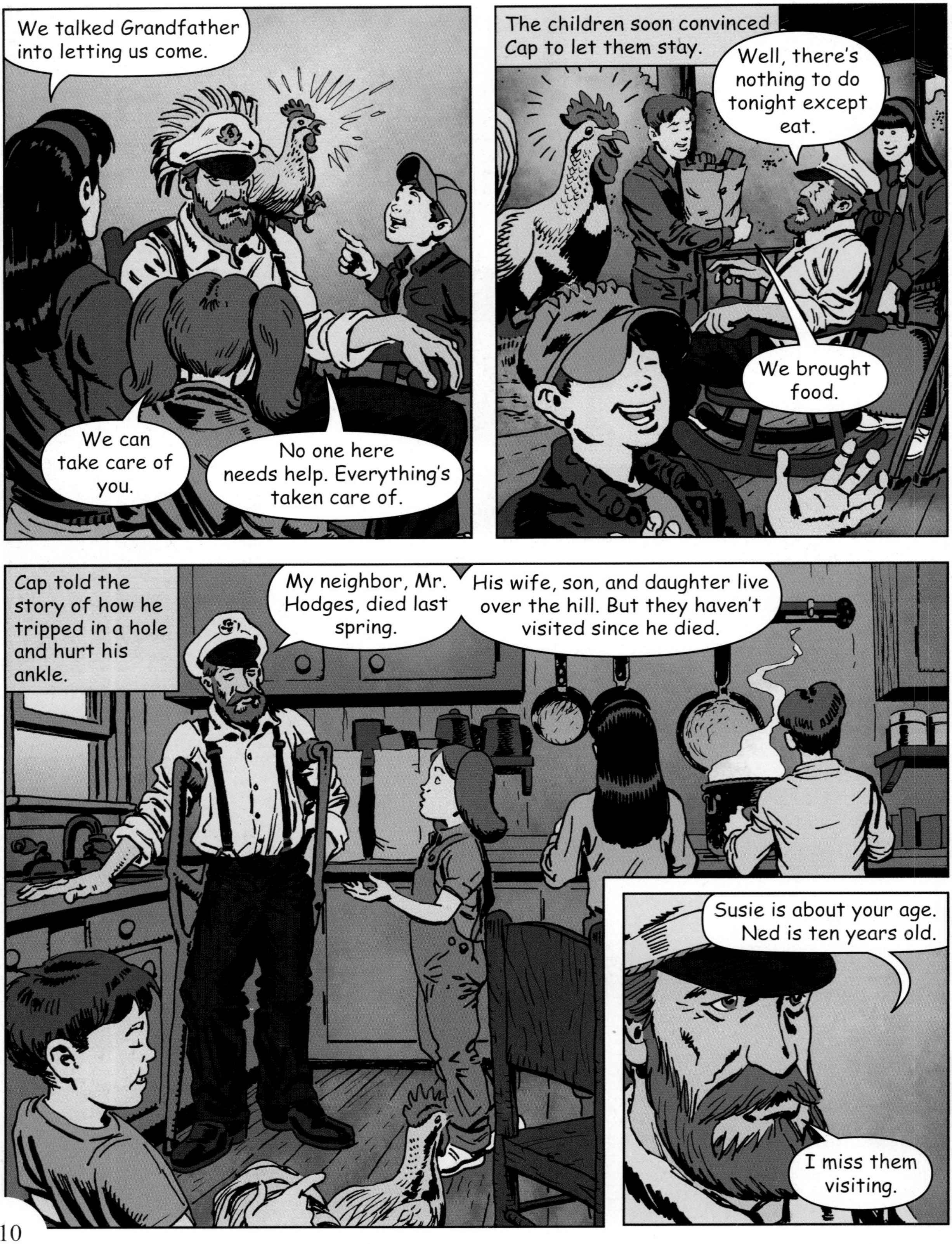
We talked Grandfather into letting us come.
We can take care of you.
No one here needs help. Everything's taken care of.
The children soon convinced Cap to let them stay.
Well, there's nothing to do tonight except eat.
We brought food.
Cap told the story of how he tripped in a hole and hurt his ankle.
My neighbor, Mr. Hodges, died last spring.
His wife, son, and daughter live over the hill. But they haven't visited since he died.
Susie is about your age. Ned is ten years old.
I miss them visiting.

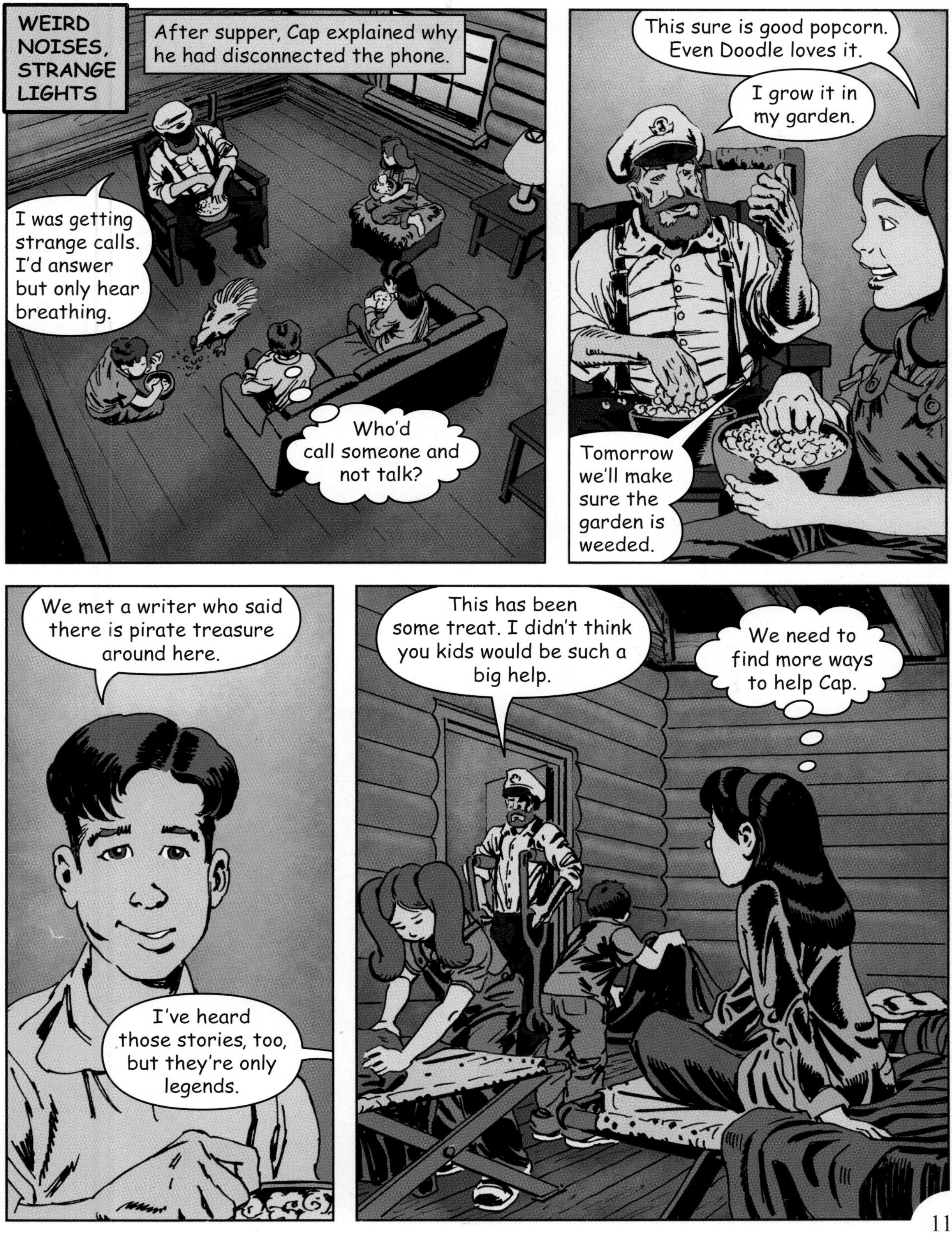
WEIRD NOISES, STRANGE LIGHTS
After supper, Cap explained why he had disconnected the phone.
I was getting strange calls. I'd answer but only hear breathing.
Who'd call someone and not talk?
This sure is good popcorn. Even Doodle loves it.
I grow it in my garden.
Tomorrow we'll make sure the garden is weeded.
We met a writer who said there is pirate treasure around here.
I've heard those stories, too, but they're only legends.
This has been some treat. I didn't think you kids would be such a big help.
We need to find more ways to help Cap.

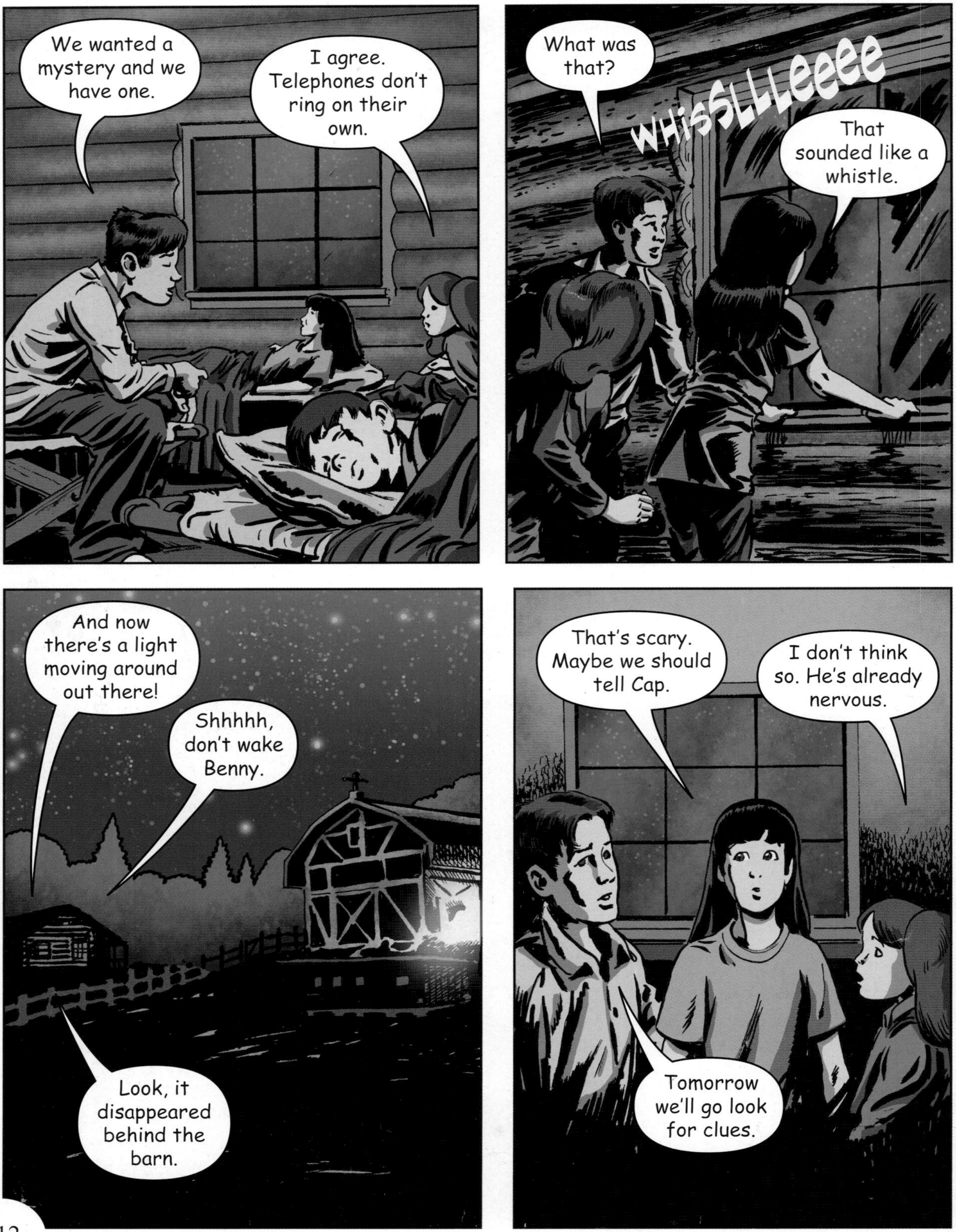
We wanted a mystery and we have one.
I agree. Telephones don't ring on their own.
What was that?
WHisSLLLeeee
That sounded like a whistle.
And now there's a light moving around out there!
Shhhhh, don't wake Benny.
Look, it disappeared behind the barn.
That's scary. Maybe we should tell Cap.
I don't think so. He's already nervous.
Tomorrow we'll go look for clues.

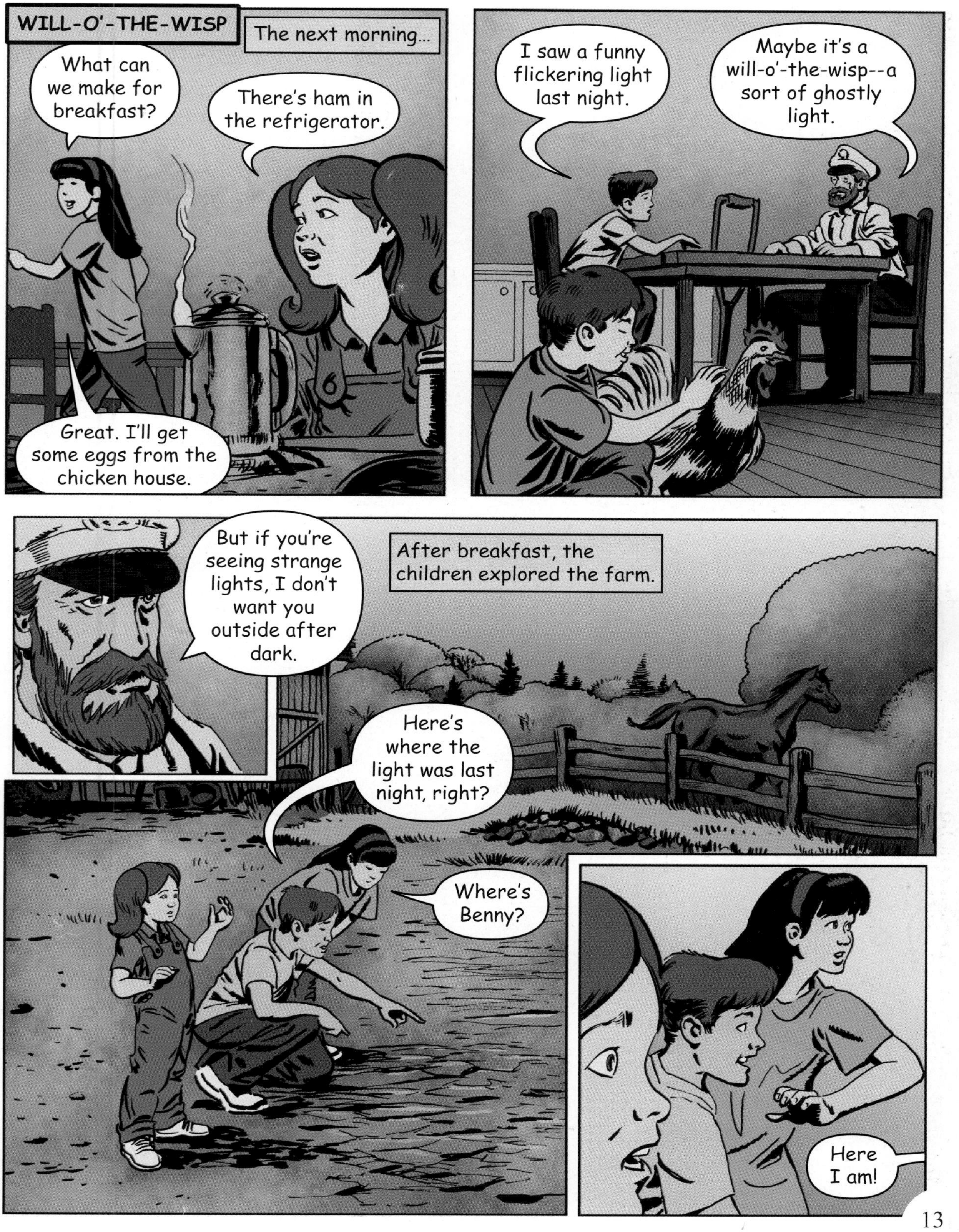
WILL-O'-THE-WISP
The next morning...
What can we make for breakfast?
There's ham in the refrigerator.
Great. I'll get some eggs from the chicken house.
I saw a funny flickering light last night.
Maybe it's a will-o'-the-wisp--a sort of ghostly light.
But if you're seeing strange lights, I don't want you outside after dark.
After breakfast, the children explored the farm.
Here's where the light was last night, right?
Where's Benny?
Here I am!

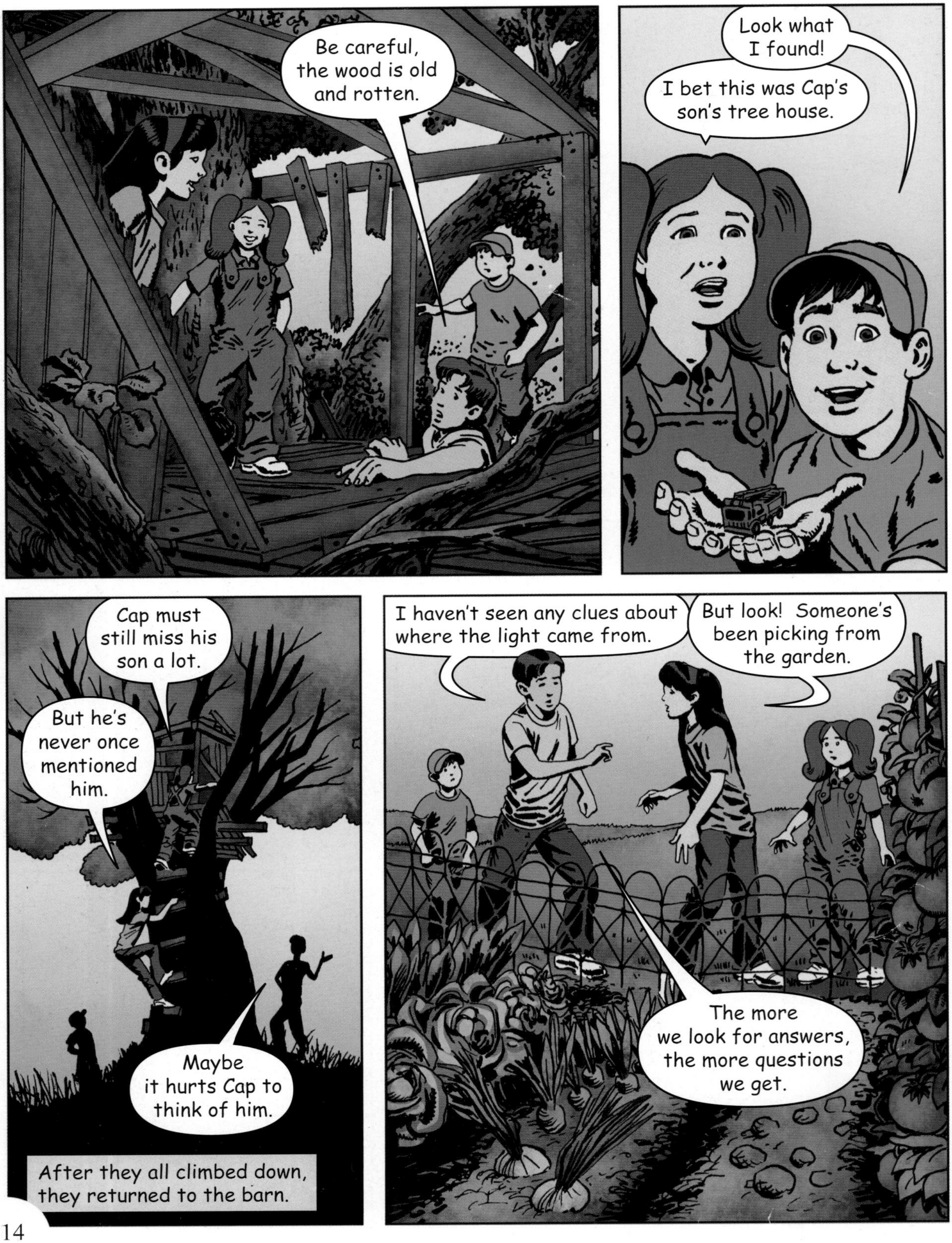
Be careful, the wood is old and rotten.
Look what I found!
I bet this was Cap's son's tree house.
Cap must still miss his son a lot.
But he's never once mentioned him.
Maybe it hurts Cap to think of him.
After they all climbed down, they returned to the barn.
I haven't seen any clues about where the light came from.
But look! Someone's been picking from the garden.
The more we look for answers, the more questions we get.

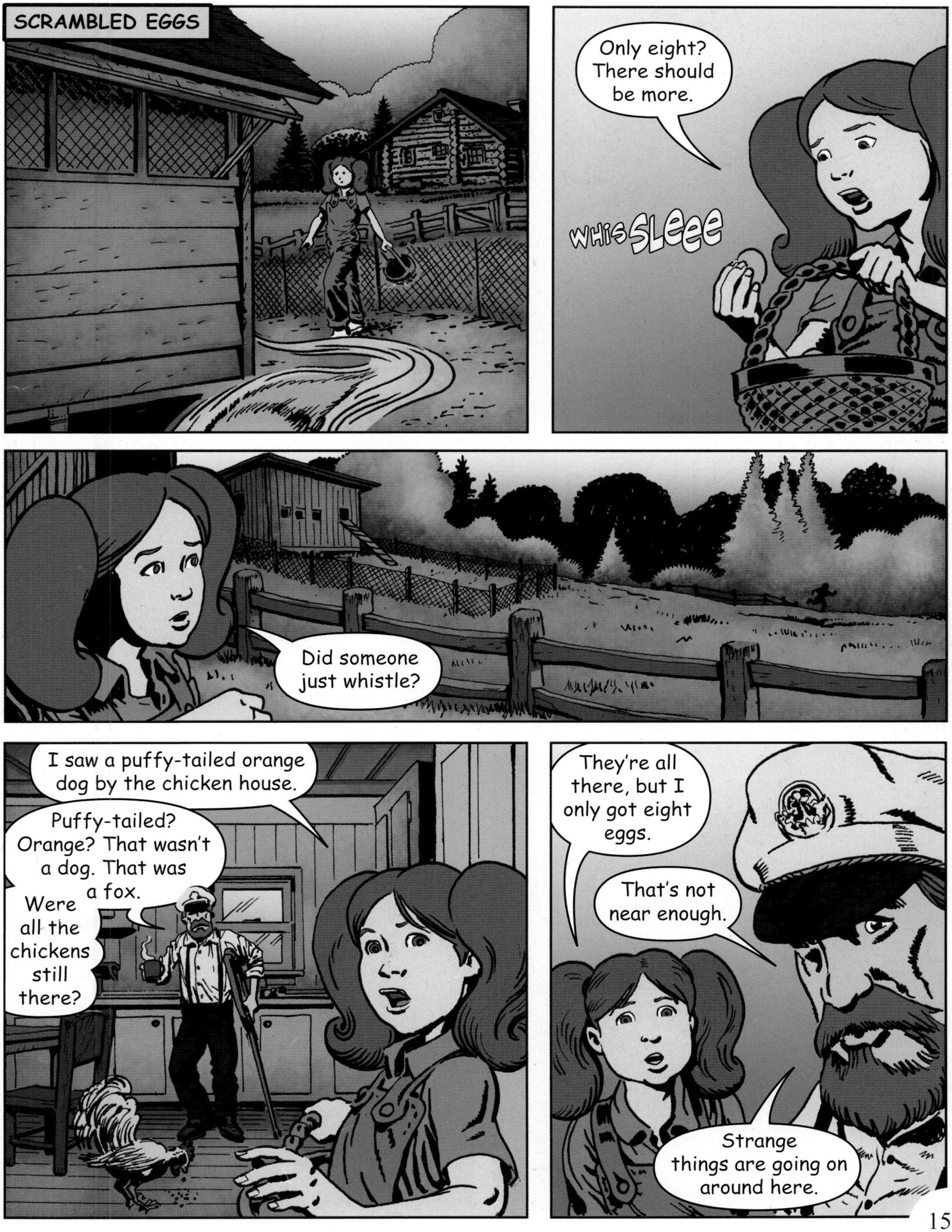
SCRAMBLED EGGS
Only eight? There should be more.
WHISSLEEE
Did someone just whistle?
I saw a puffy-tailed orange dog by the chicken house.
Puffy-tailed? Orange? That wasn't a dog. That was a fox.
Were all the chickens still there?
They're all there, but I only got eight eggs.
That's not near enough.
Strange things are going on around here.

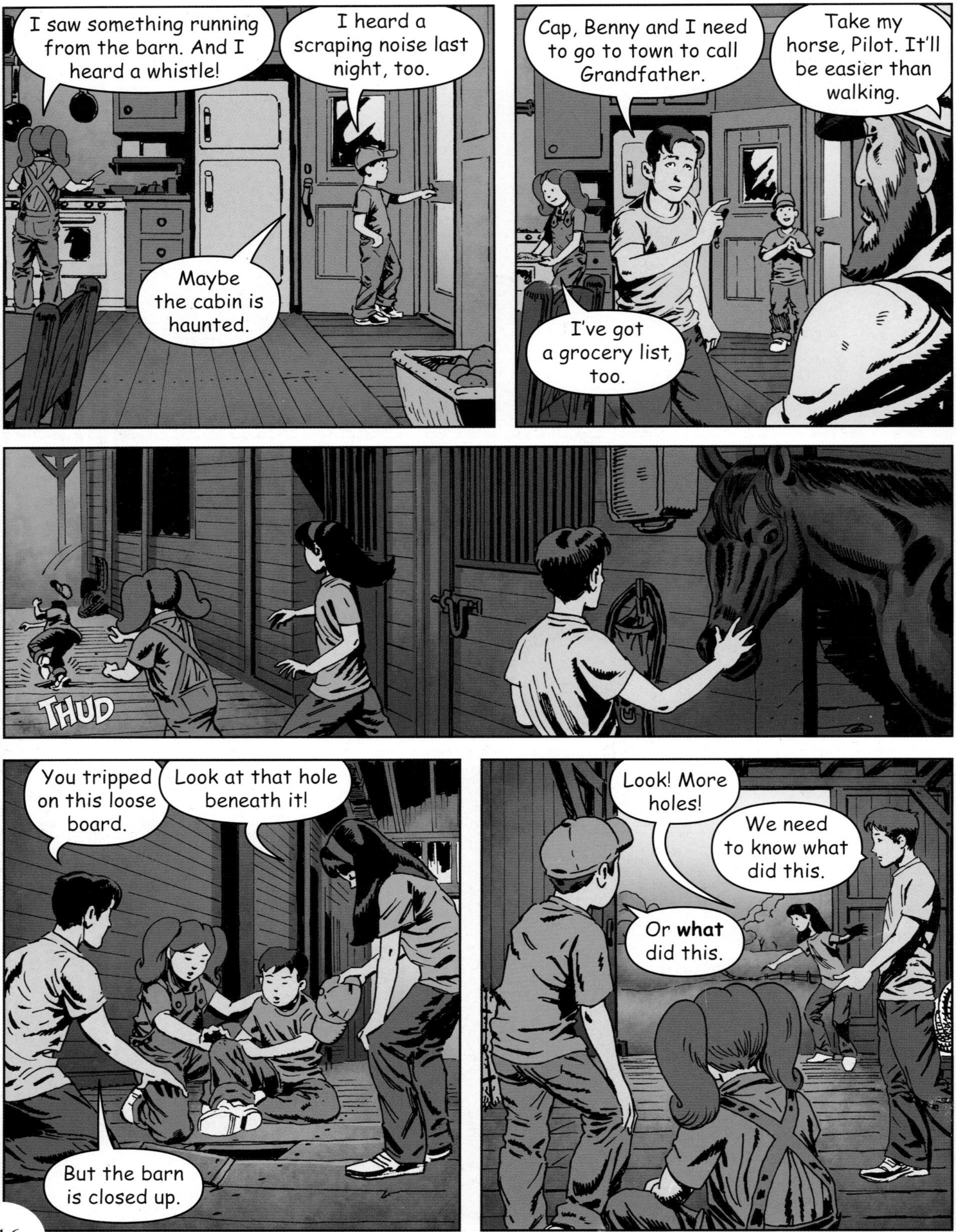
I saw something running from the barn. And I heard a whistle!
I heard a scraping noise last night, too.
Maybe the cabin is haunted.
Cap, Benny and I need to go to town to call Grandfather.
Take my horse, Pilot. It'll be easier than walking.
I've got a grocery list, too.
THUD
You tripped on this loose board.
Look at that hole beneath it!
But the barn is closed up.
Look! More holes!
We need to know what did this.
Or **what** did this.

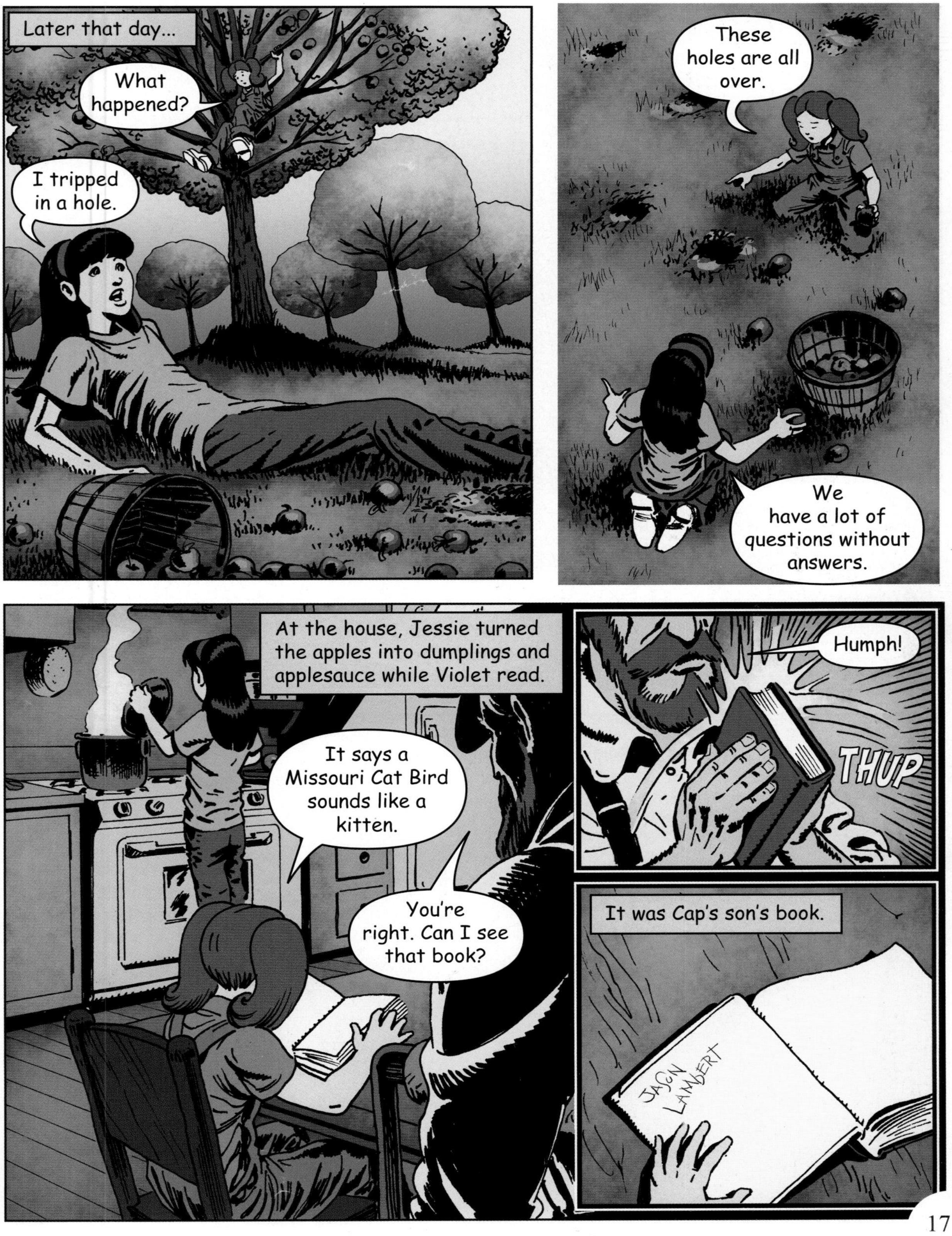

Later that day...
What happened?
I tripped in a hole.
These holes are all over.
We have a lot of questions without answers.
At the house, Jessie turned the apples into dumplings and applesauce while Violet read.
It says a Missouri Cat Bird sounds like a kitten.
You're right. Can I see that book?
Humph!
THUP
It was Cap's son's book.
JASON LAMBERT

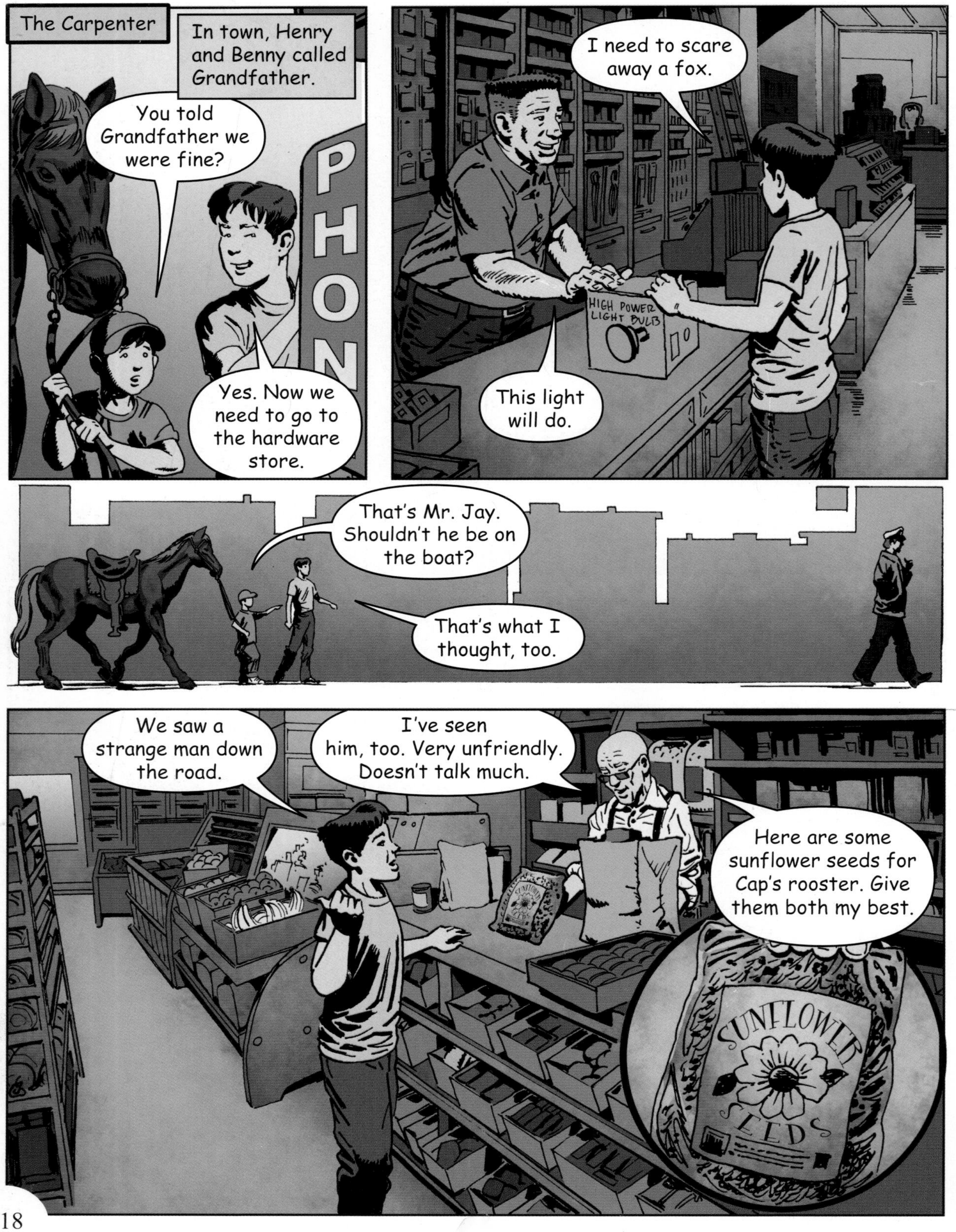

The Carpenter
In town, Henry and Benny called Grandfather.
You told Grandfather we were fine?
PHON
Yes. Now we need to go to the hardware store.
I need to scare away a fox.
HIGH POWER LIGHT BULB
This light will do.
That's Mr. Jay. Shouldn't he be on the boat?
That's what I thought, too.
We saw a strange man down the road.
I've seen him, too. Very unfriendly. Doesn't talk much.
Here are some sunflower seeds for Cap's rooster. Give them both my best.
SUNFLOWER SEEDS

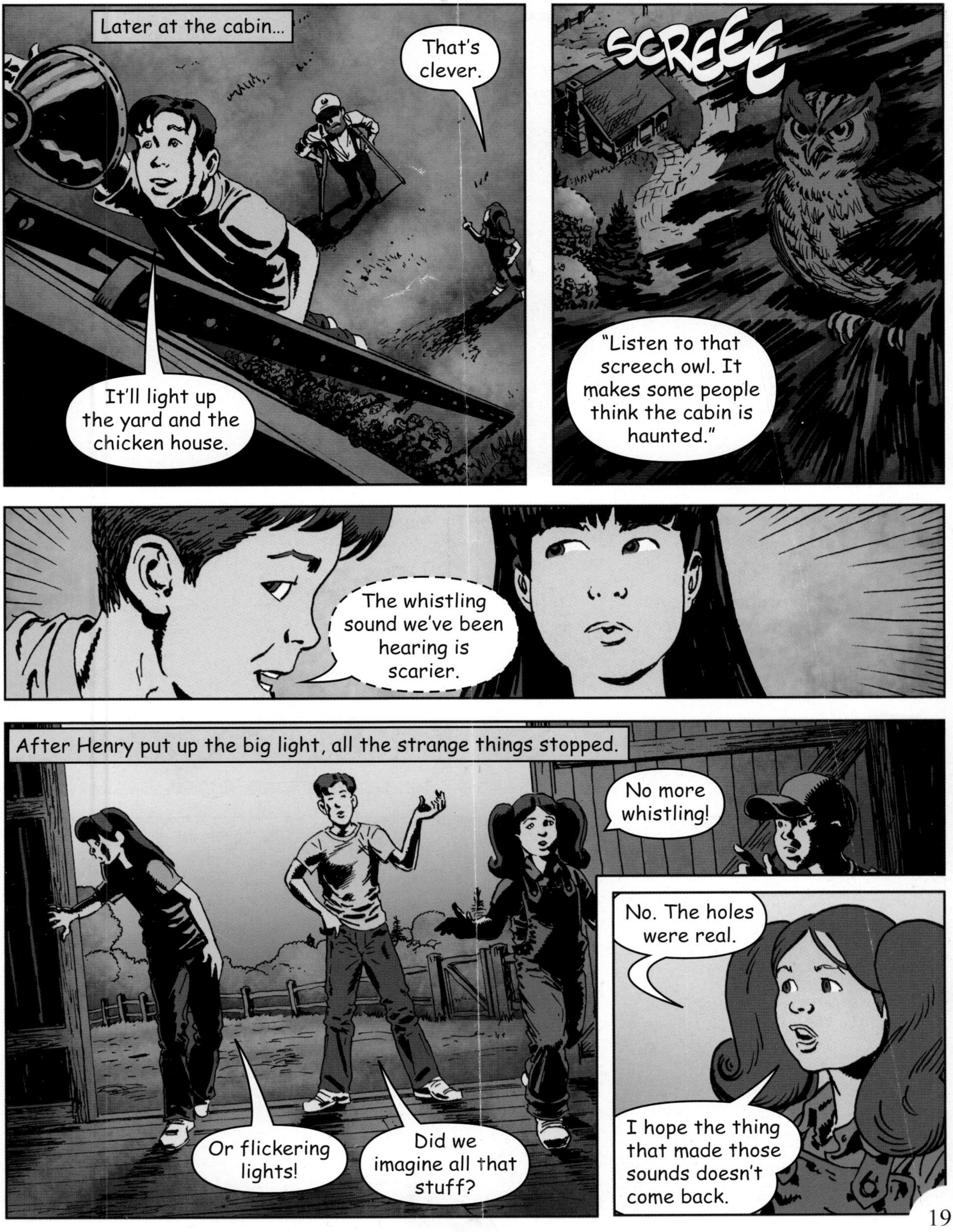
Later at the cabin...
That's clever.
It'll light up the yard and the chicken house.
SCREEE
"Listen to that screech owl. It makes some people think the cabin is haunted."
The whistling sound we've been hearing is scarier.
After Henry put up the big light, all the strange things stopped.
No more whistling!
Or flickering lights!
Did we imagine all that stuff?
No. The holes were real.
I hope the thing that made those sounds doesn't come back.

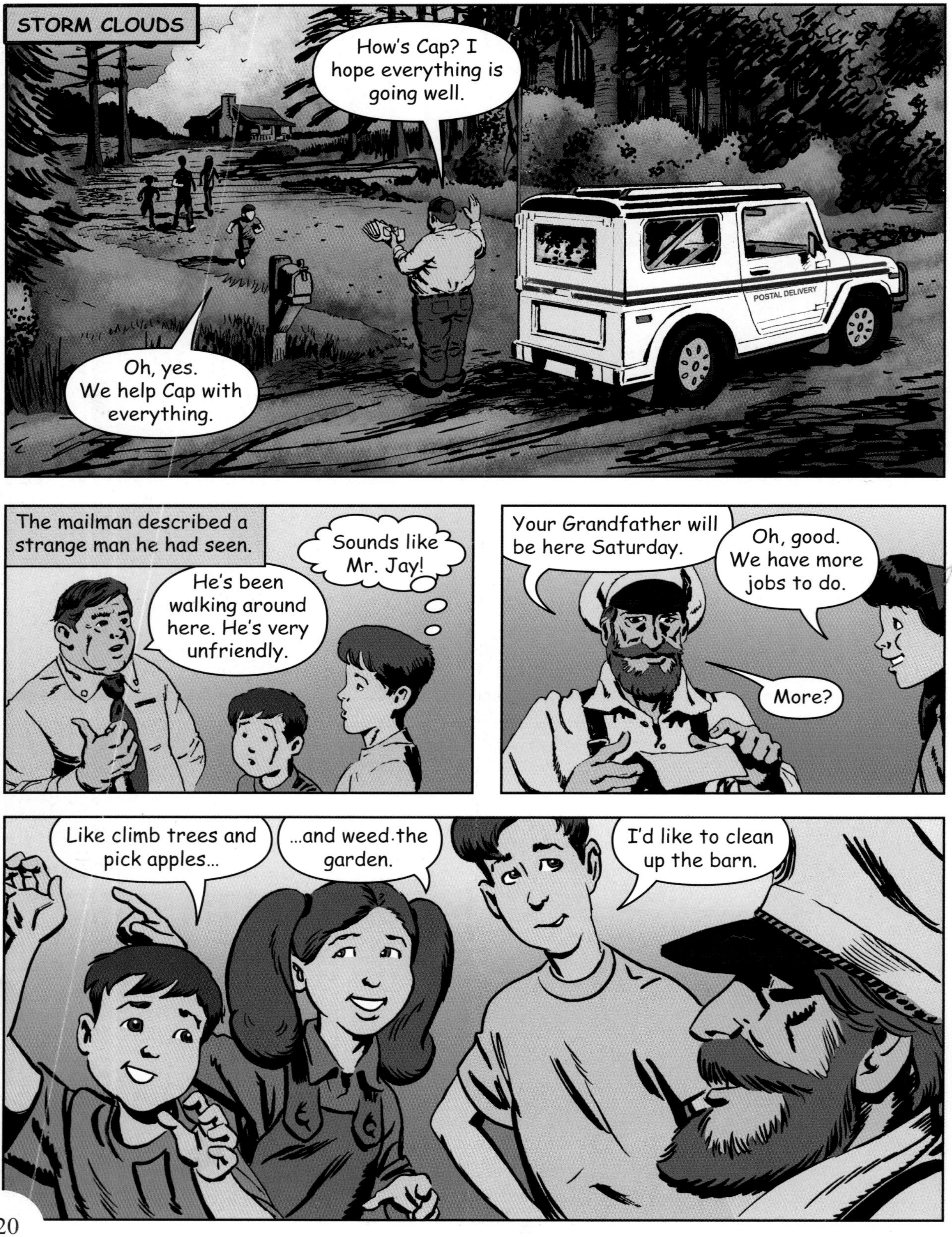
STORM CLOUDS
How's Cap? I hope everything is going well.
POSTAL DELIVERY
Oh, yes. We help Cap with everything.
The mailman described a strange man he had seen.
He's been walking around here. He's very unfriendly.
Sounds like Mr. Jay!
Your Grandfather will be here Saturday.
Oh, good. We have more jobs to do.
More?
Like climb trees and pick apples...
...and weed the garden.
I'd like to clean up the barn.

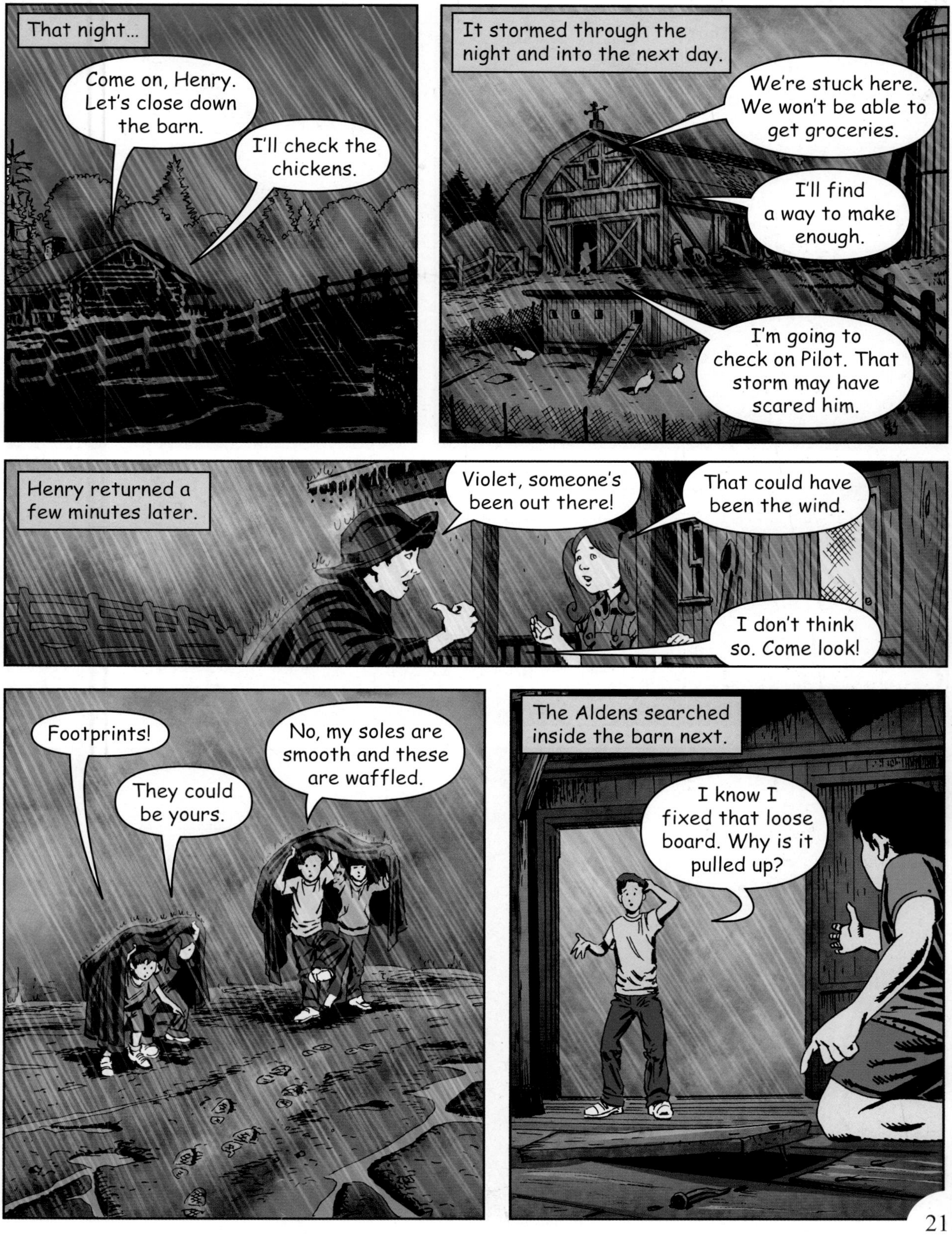
That night...
Come on, Henry. Let's close down the barn.
I'll check the chickens.
It stormed through the night and into the next day.
We're stuck here. We won't be able to get groceries.
I'll find a way to make enough.
I'm going to check on Pilot. That storm may have scared him.
Henry returned a few minutes later.
Violet, someone's been out there!
That could have been the wind.
I don't think so. Come look!
Footprints!
They could be yours.
No, my soles are smooth and these are waffled.
The Aldens searched inside the barn next.
I know I fixed that loose board. Why is it pulled up?

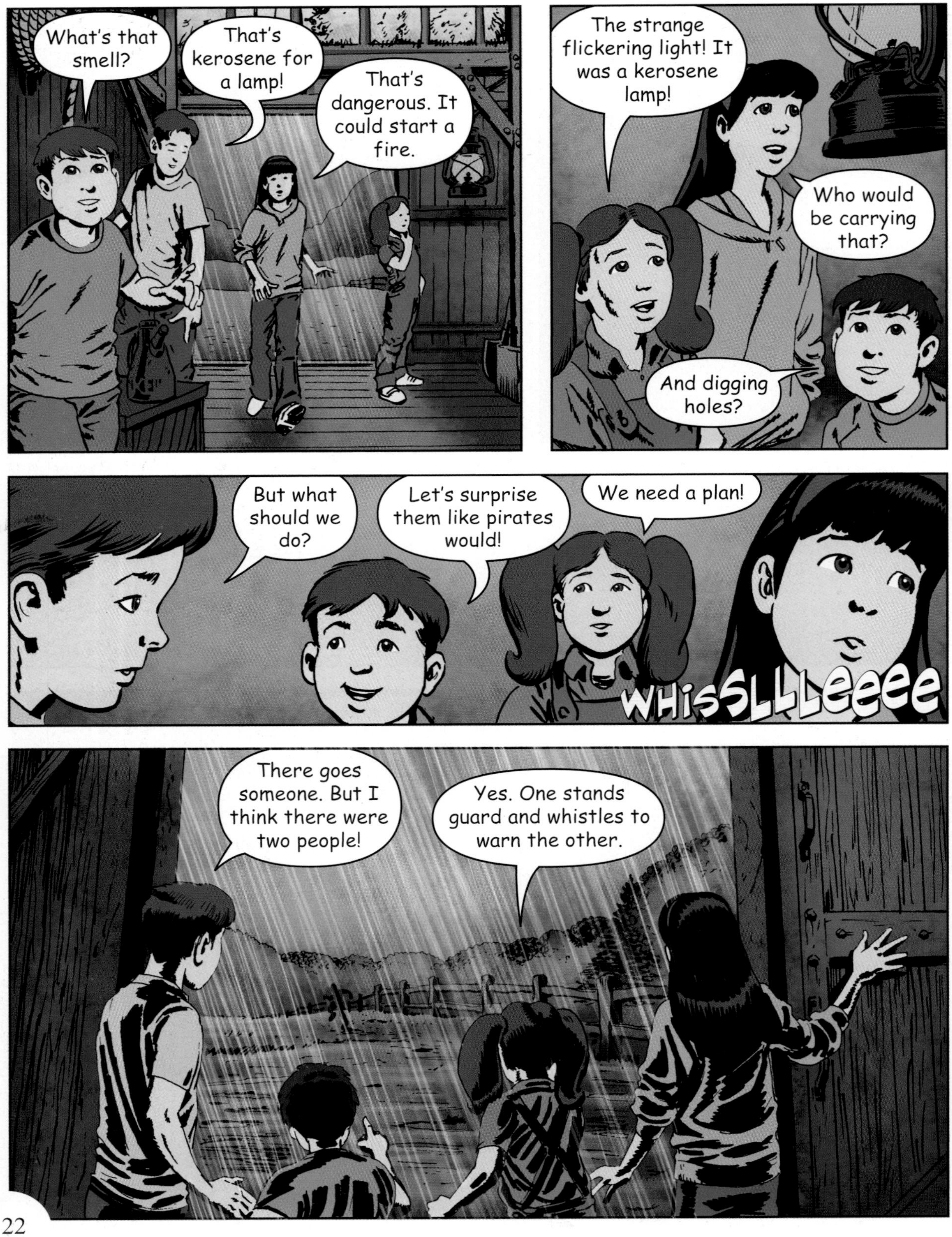
What's that smell?
That's kerosene for a lamp!
That's dangerous. It could start a fire.
The strange flickering light! It was a kerosene lamp!
Who would be carrying that?
And digging holes?
But what should we do?
Let's surprise them like pirates would!
We need a plan!
WHisSLLLeeee
There goes someone. But I think there were two people!
Yes. One stands guard and whistles to warn the other.

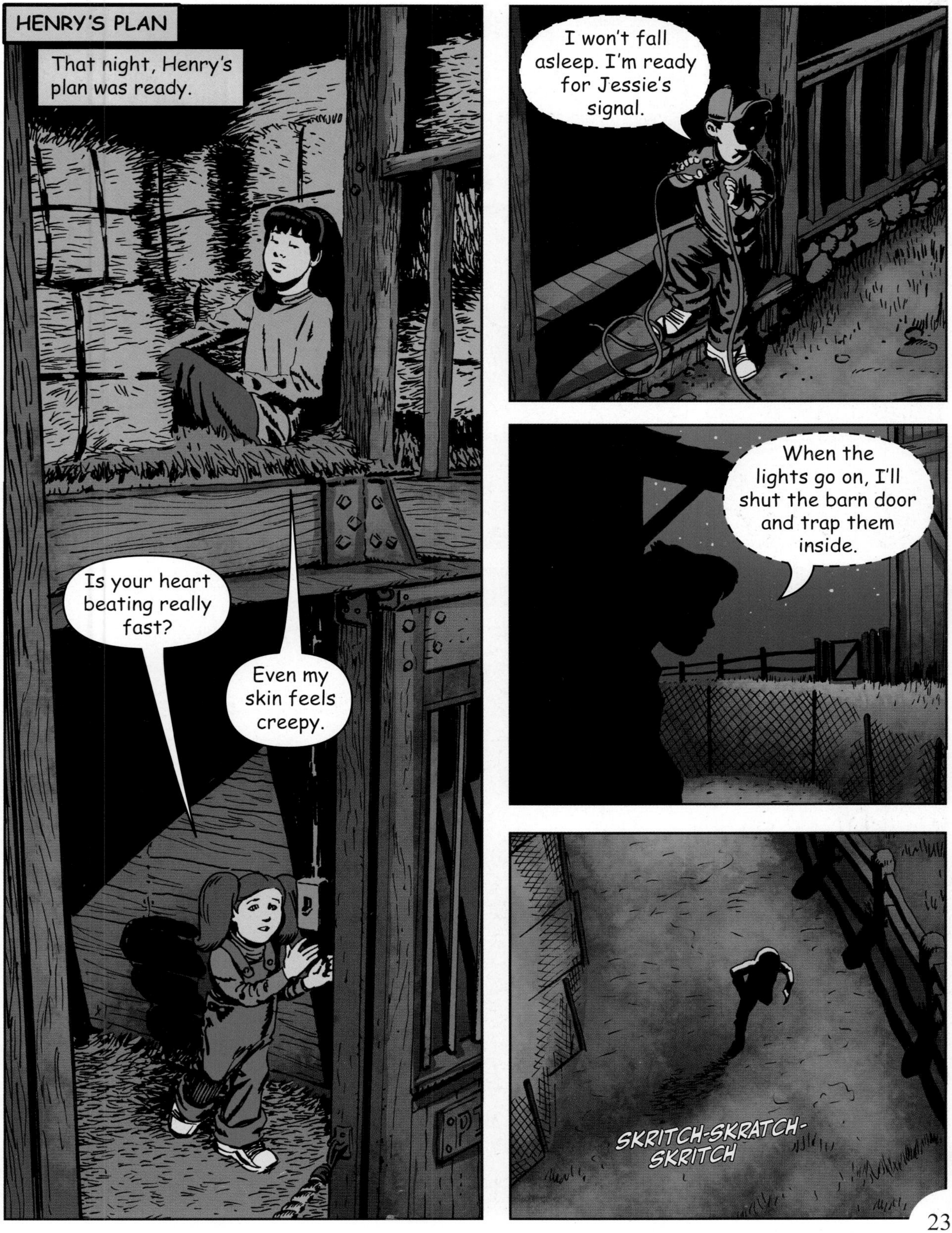
HENRY'S PLAN
That night, Henry's plan was ready.
Is your heart beating really fast?
Even my skin feels creepy.
I won't fall asleep. I'm ready for Jessie's signal.
When the lights go on, I'll shut the barn door and trap them inside.
SKRITCH-SKRATCH-SKRITCH

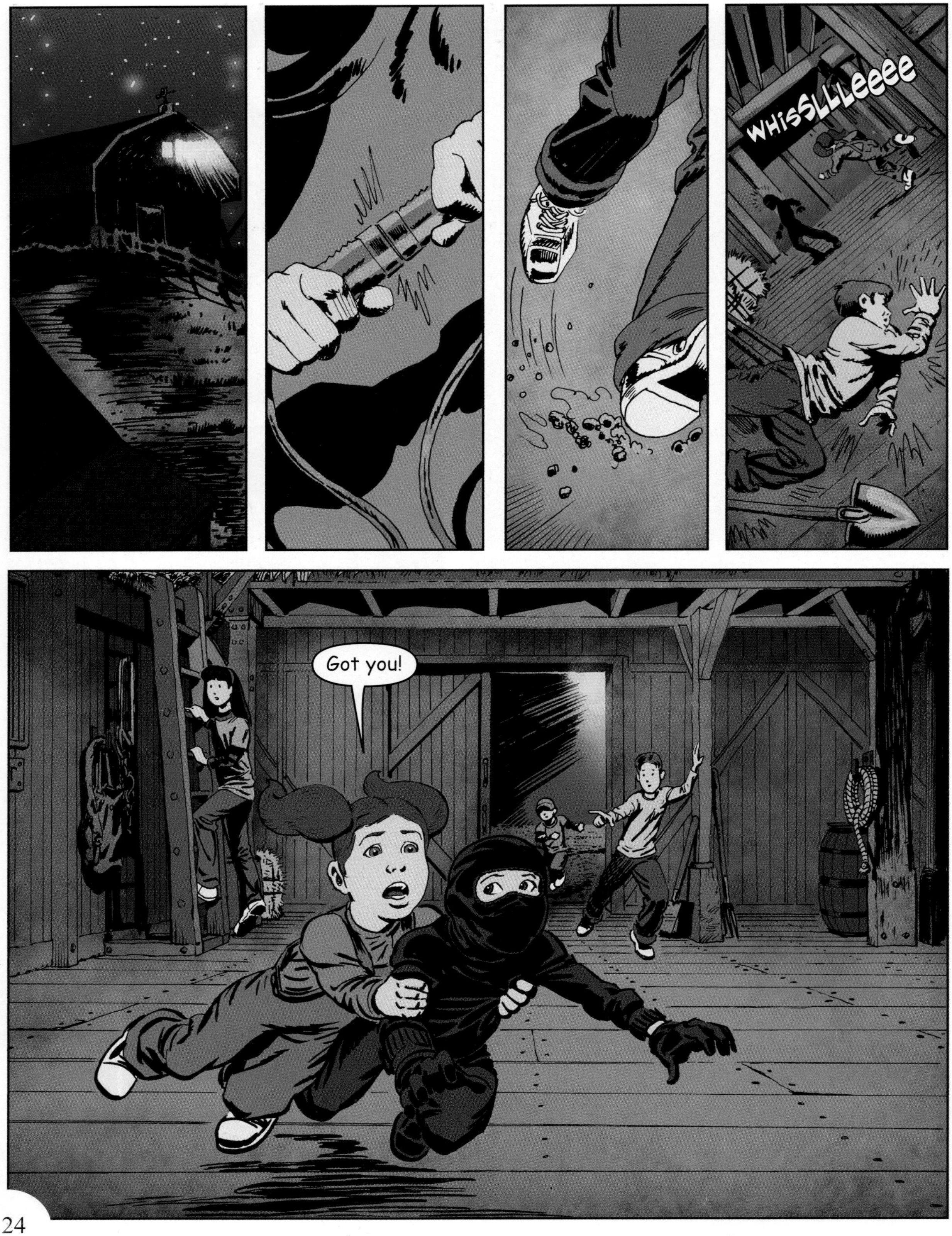
WHisSLLLeeee
Got you!

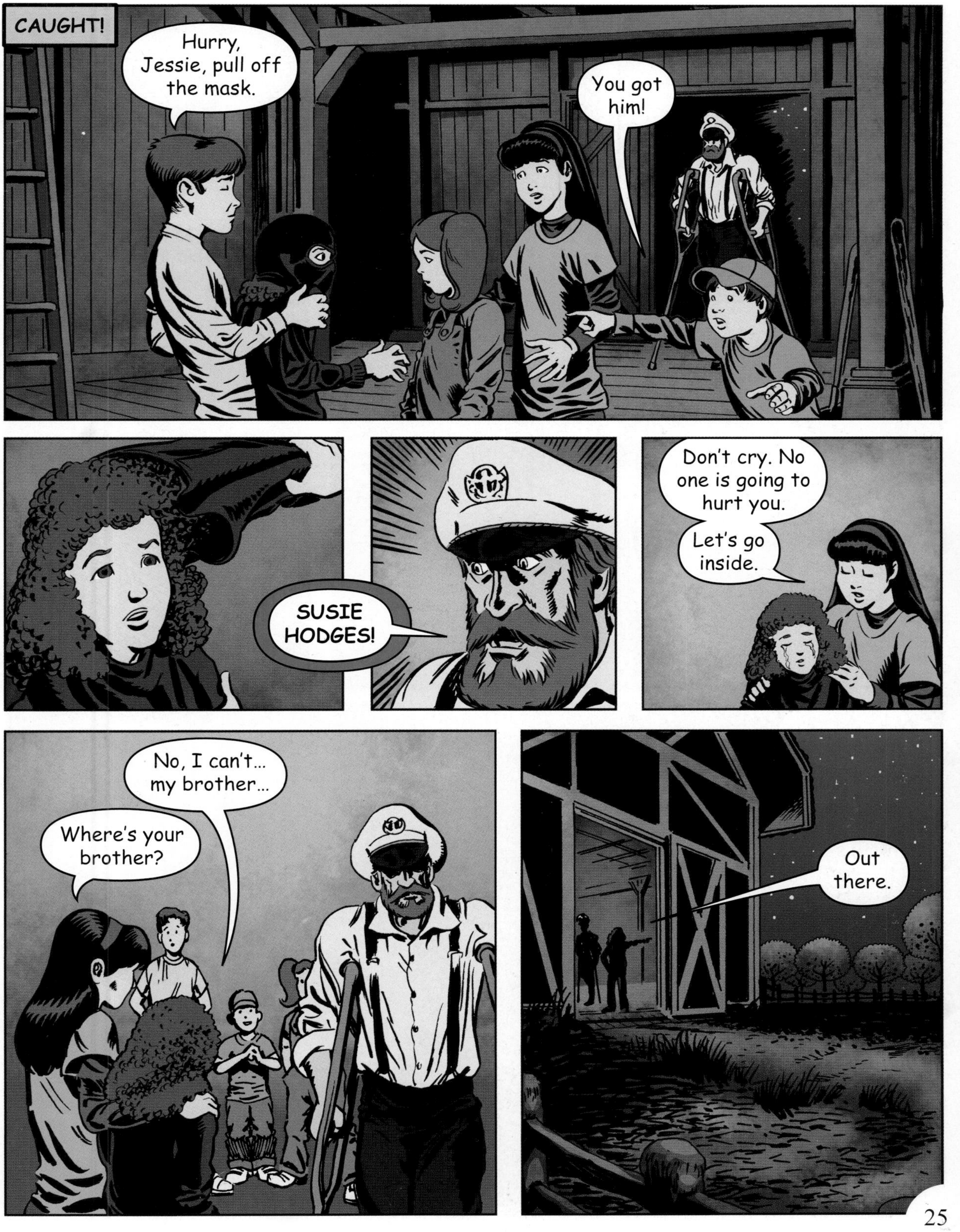
CAUGHT!
Hurry, Jessie, pull off the mask.
You got him!
SUSIE HODGES!
Don't cry. No one is going to hurt you.
Let's go inside.
No, I can't... my brother...
Where's your brother?
Out there.

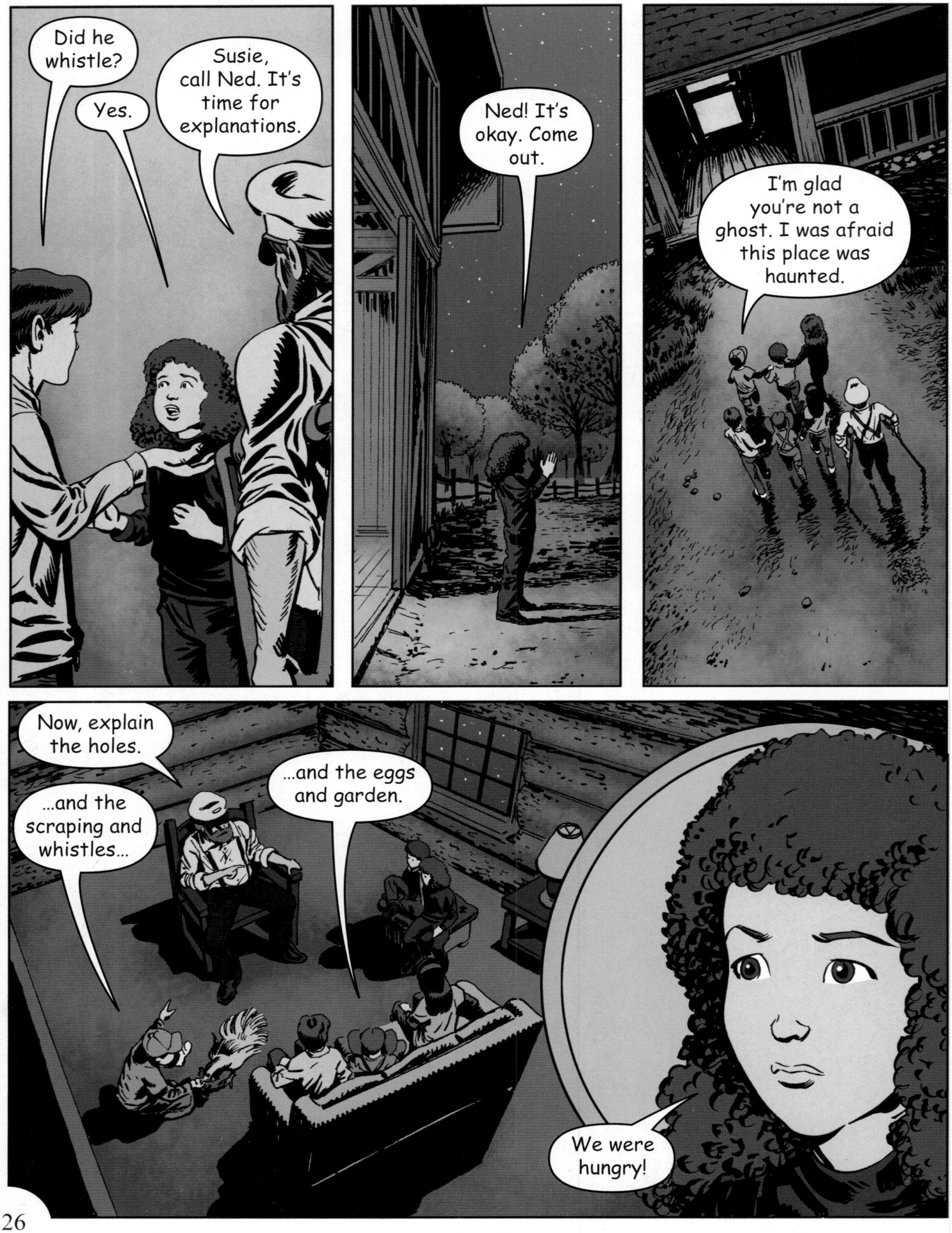
Did he whistle?
Yes.
Susie, call Ned. It's time for explanations.
Ned! It's okay. Come out.
I'm glad you're not a ghost. I was afraid this place was haunted.
Now, explain the holes.
...and the scraping and whistles...
...and the eggs and garden.
We were hungry!

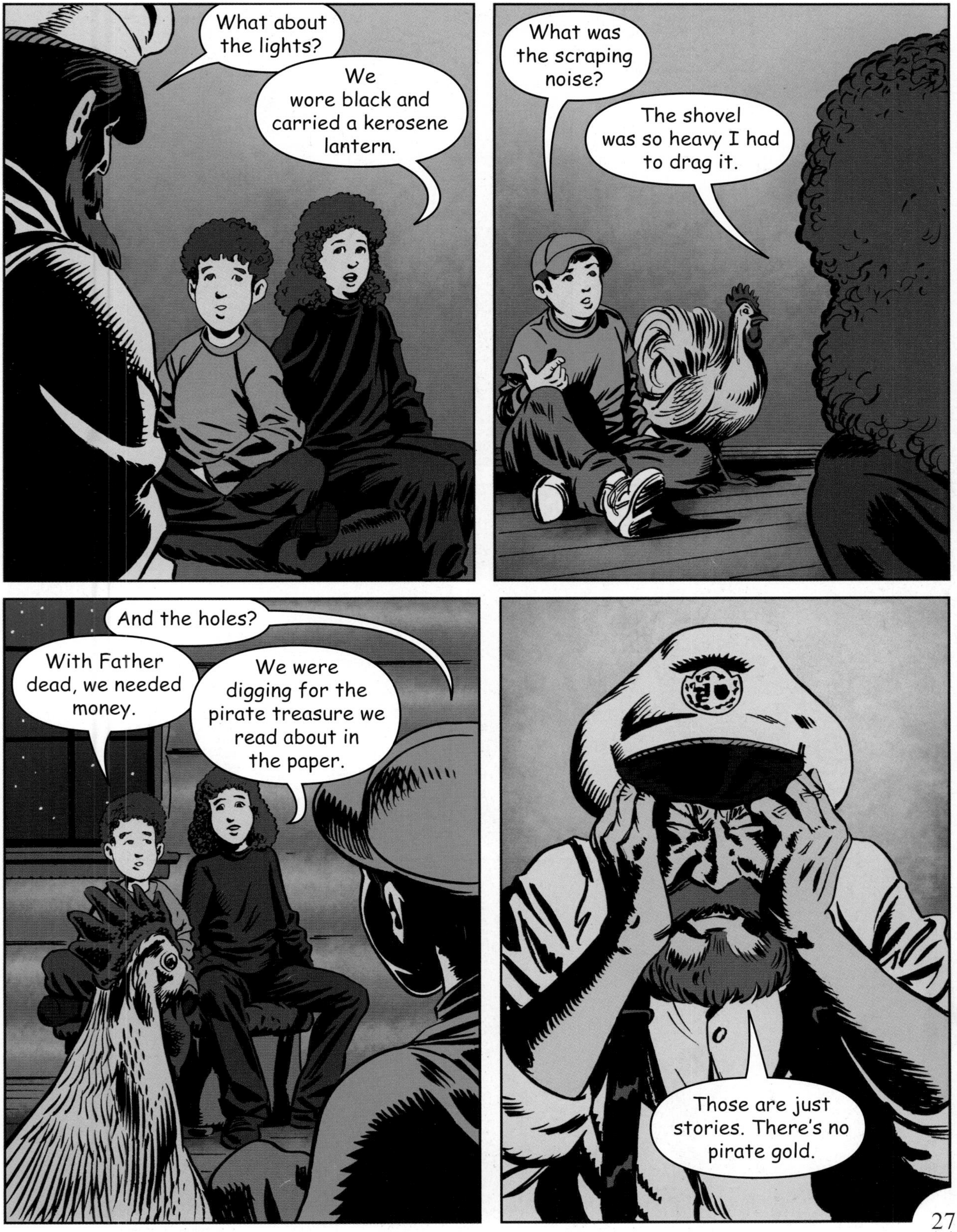
What about the lights?
We wore black and carried a kerosene lantern.
What was the scraping noise?
The shovel was so heavy I had to drag it.
And the holes?
With Father dead, we needed money.
We were digging for the pirate treasure we read about in the paper.
Those are just stories. There's no pirate gold.

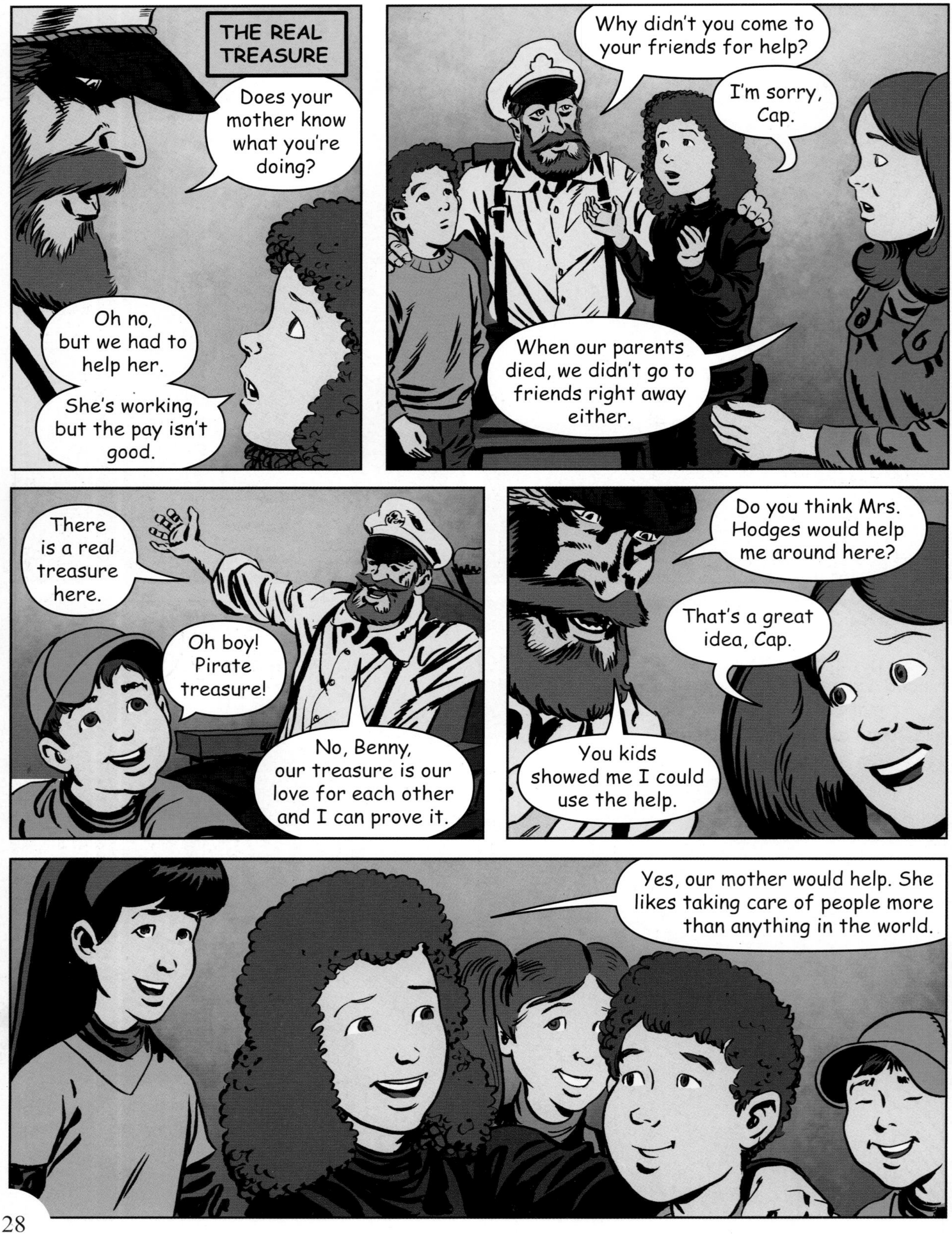
THE REAL TREASURE
Does your mother know what you're doing?
Oh no, but we had to help her.
She's working, but the pay isn't good.
Why didn't you come to your friends for help?
I'm sorry, Cap.
When our parents died, we didn't go to friends right away either.
There is a real treasure here.
Oh boy! Pirate treasure!
No, Benny, our treasure is our love for each other and I can prove it.
Do you think Mrs. Hodges would help me around here?
That's a great idea, Cap.
You kids showed me I could use the help.
Yes, our mother would help. She likes taking care of people more than anything in the world.

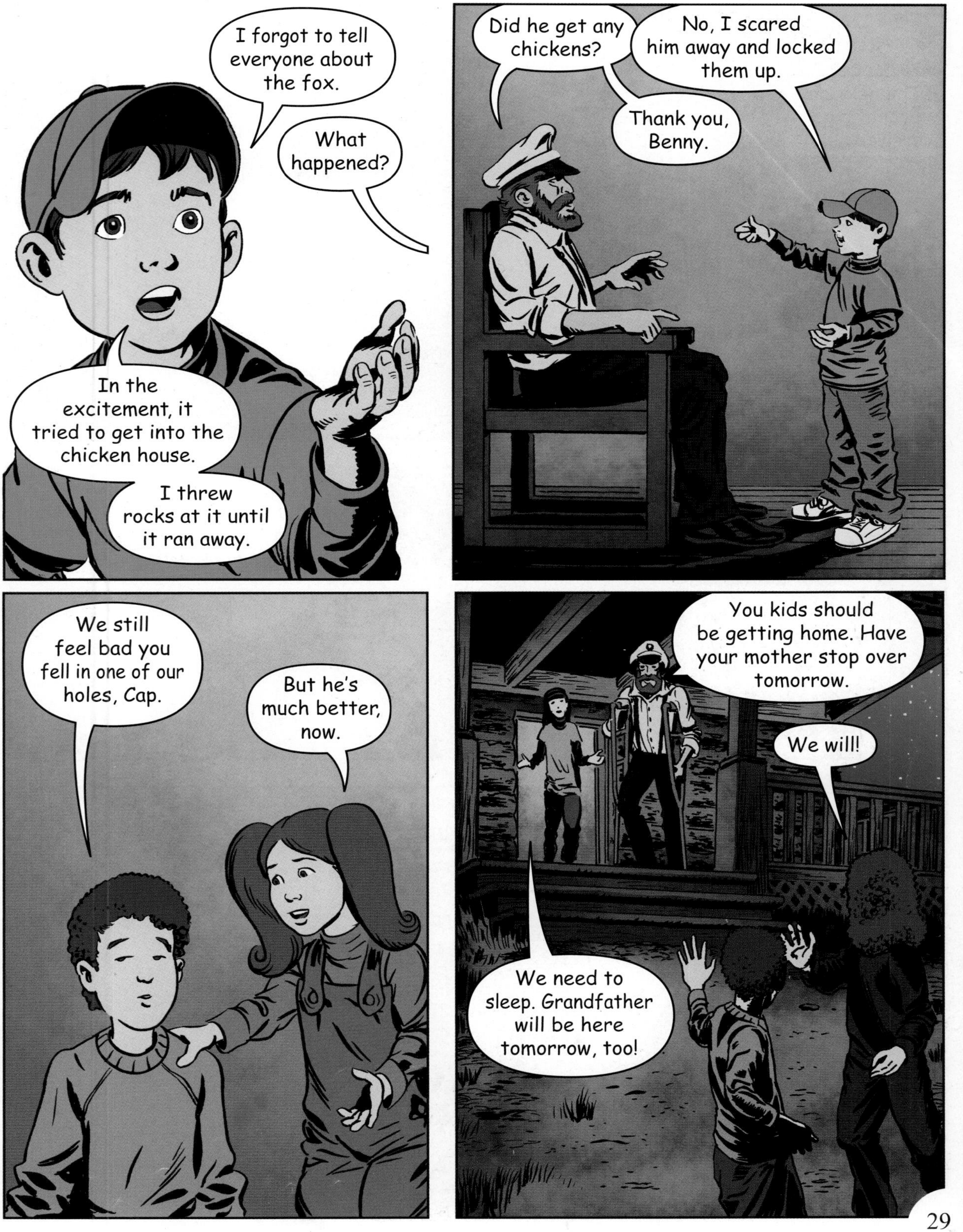
I forgot to tell everyone about the fox.
What happened?
In the excitement, it tried to get into the chicken house.
I threw rocks at it until it ran away.
Did he get any chickens?
No, I scared him away and locked them up.
Thank you, Benny.
We still feel bad you fell in one of our holes, Cap.
But he's much better, now.
You kids should be getting home. Have your mother stop over tomorrow.
We will!
We need to sleep. Grandfather will be here tomorrow, too!

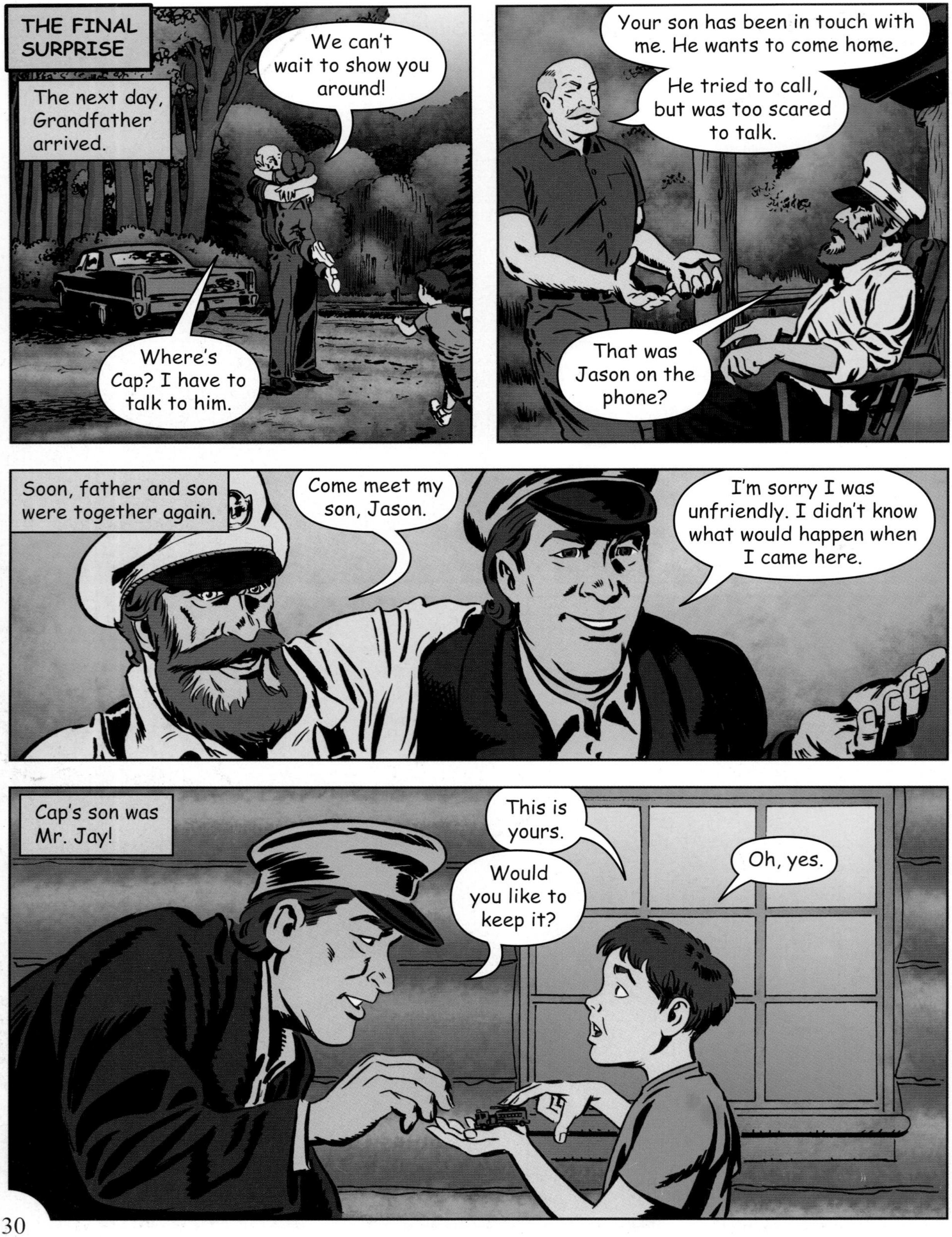
THE FINAL SURPRISE
The next day, Grandfather arrived.
We can't wait to show you around!
Where's Cap? I have to talk to him.
Your son has been in touch with me. He wants to come home.
He tried to call, but was too scared to talk.
That was Jason on the phone?
Soon, father and son were together again.
Come meet my son, Jason.
I'm sorry I was unfriendly. I didn't know what would happen when I came here.
Cap's son was Mr. Jay!
This is yours.
Would you like to keep it?
Oh, yes.

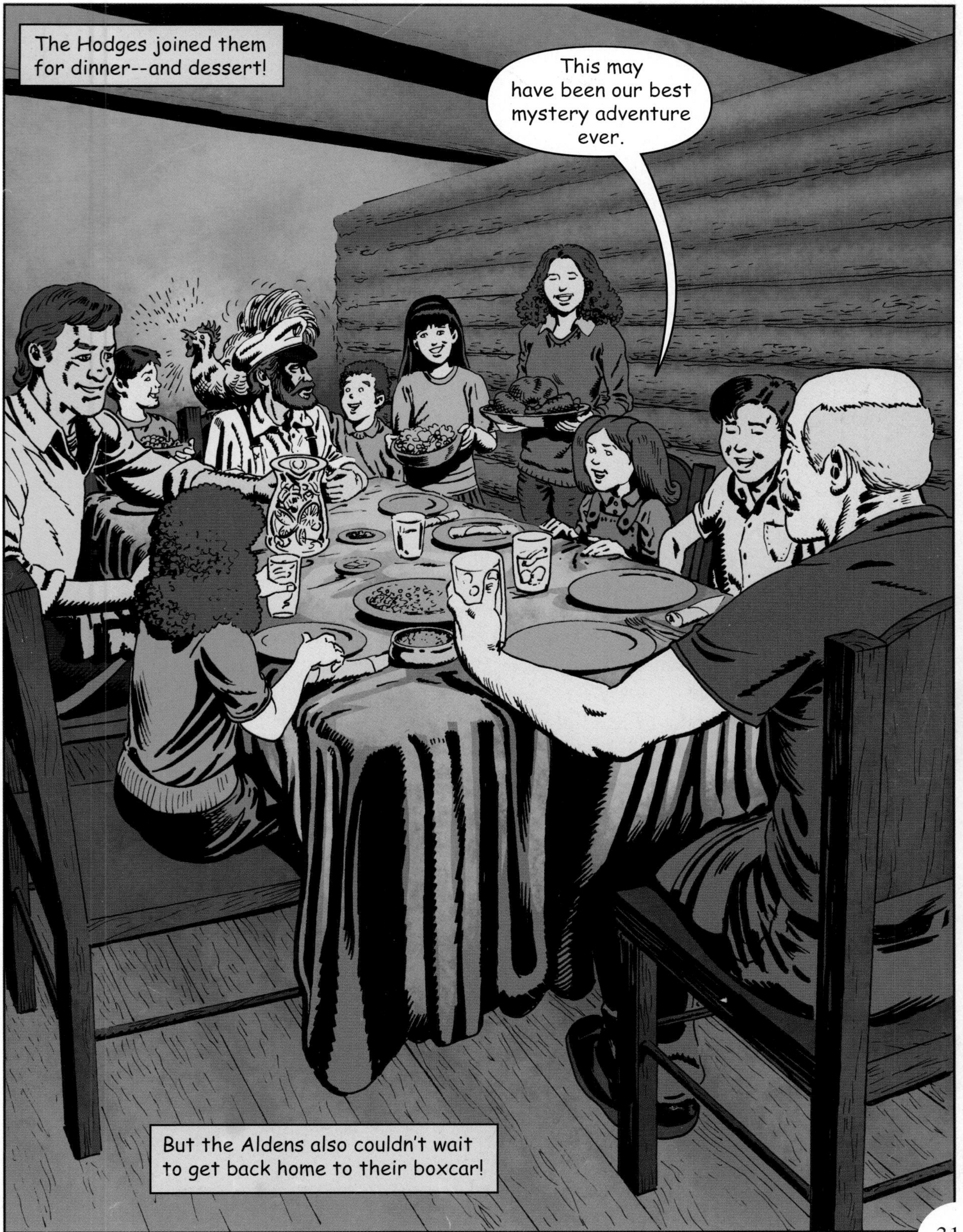
The Hodges joined them for dinner--and dessert!
This may have been our best mystery adventure ever.
But the Aldens also couldn't wait to get back home to their boxcar!

ABOUT THE CREATOR

Gertrude Chandler Warner was born on April 16, 1890, in Putnam, Connecticut. In 1918, Warner began teaching at Israel Putnam School. As a teacher, she discovered that many readers who liked an exciting story could not find books that were both easy and fun to read. She decided to try to meet this need. In 1942, *The Boxcar Children* was published for these readers.

Warner drew on her own experience to write *The Boxcar Children.* As a child she spent hours watching trains go by on the tracks near her family home. She often dreamed about what it would be like to live in a caboose or freight car—just as the Alden children do.

When readers asked for more Alden adventures, Warner began additional stories. While the mystery element is central to each of the books, she never thought of them as strictly juvenile mysteries. She liked to stress the Aldens' independence. Henry, Jessie, Violet, and Benny go about most of their adventures with as little adult supervision as possible—something that delights young readers.

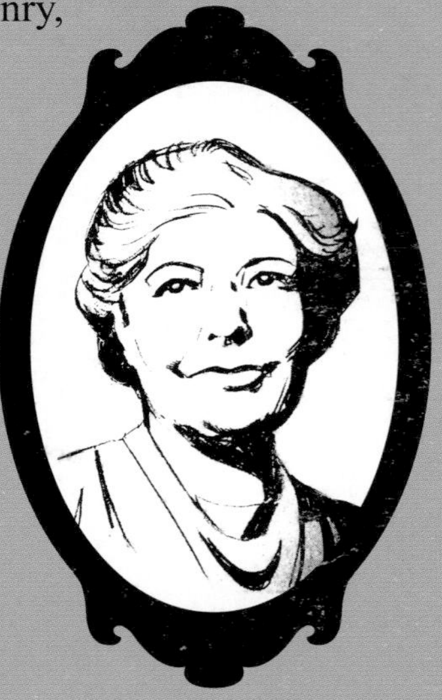

During her lifetime, Warner received hundreds of letters from fans as she continued the Aldens' adventures, writing nineteen Boxcar Children books in all. After her death in 1979, her publisher, Albert Whitman and Company, carried on Warner's vision. Today, the Boxcar Children series has more than 100 books.